THE DARLINGTON ROGUE

THE DARLINGTON ROGUE

**THE SECOND BOOK IN
"THE CONCH CONVERSION" TRILOGY**

J.N Sadler

Copyright © 2021 J.N Sadler.

All rights reserved. No part of this book may be reproduced in any form or by any electronic or mechanical means, including information storage and retrieval systems, without permission in writing from the publisher, except by reviewers, who may quote brief passages in a review.

ISBN: 978-1-63795-430-0   (Paperback Edition)
ISBN: 978-1-63795-431-7   (Hardcover Edition)
ISBN: 978-1-63795-429-4   (E-book Edition)

Some characters and events in this book are fictitious. Any similarity to real persons, living or dead, is coincidental and not intended by the author.

Book Ordering Information

Phone Number: 315 288-7939 ext. 1000 or 347-901-4920
Email: info@globalsummithouse.com
Global Summit House
www.globalsummithouse.com

Printed in the United States of America

Contents

Chapter 1:	The Air Show	1
Chapter 2:	A Bigger Boat	6
Chapter 3:	Nara's Place	8
Chapter 4:	The Dream Team	11
Chapter 5:	The Day of Departure	16
Chapter 6:	Ready to Go	23
Chapter 7:	The Entrance to the Rogue	38
Chapter 8:	The Unfamiliar	46
Chapter 9:	Conversation with Evo-Scientists	51
Chapter 10:	Home	62

Chapter 1

The Air Show

Experimental aircraft took turns flying over the air field where Buck Martin was the feature flyer. A large crowd had gathered. Necks craned to watch the stunts of the Piper Cubs and other antique models fly by. The air clown played balance games on the wings of the Bamboo Bomber and pretended to fall, only to climb back up in the wind, hanging on the tip of the wing by a few fingers.

It was announced that Buck was going to do some aero ballet with his Navy jet, after which would follow the famous Blue Angels, in formation. The Christen Eagle taxied and parked on the green grass field next to a fabric-covered Cessna whose wing-walker was 89 years old. Then there was Tom's favorite plane, Boeing's Navy Stearman, a double-wing, open-cockpit antique, retired from World War II and re-painted red and white, given the famous name, Red Baron. Most of them now were used for crop dusters and aerobatic stunts at shows such as this.

Buck was going to surprise the audience with his own dangerous stunts: loops, aileron rolls, barrel rolls, falling leaf and Immelman turn, ending in a breathtaking nose dive. It was saved as the last event. He would fly up and out from the trees and shock them all.

Tom, one of the enthusiastic fans, continued to watch the fly-by. The sky was diminished by the passing of the gigantic water-bomber, the rare Martin Mars flying boat, last of its kind. He walked up to "Fifi", the world's only flying B-29 Super Fortress, sponsored by the Commemorative Air Force.

The afternoon sun was hot. He continued on to the water ice stand and got himself a mango cone. The last plane had parked far away at the end of the field. As the crowd mingled and drifted from plane to plane, getting autographs and pictures of the participating pilots, out of nowhere rose the Red Baron. Buck was going to perform his dangerous and novel stunts, never before tried. He set the plane on autopilot when it was at a safe altitude and shut off the engine. It went into a double hammerhead, which made it spiral speedily to the ground. He misjudged his distance, and when he tried to pull up the stick, he couldn't. It was old. It jammed as he plummeted at a hellish pace to the middle of the field. Smoke poured from the engine, which roared loudly until the explosion sounded when it hit the ground. Parts flew in all directions, and smoke billowed around the broken frame of the plane. The pilot's flaming, dismembered body was thrown out of the cockpit before its collision with the earth. The crowd was in awe. People ran towards the disaster. Tom ran as fast as he could to help, but it was obvious that the pilot could not have survived. He volunteered to assist the medics and the police. Fire trucks roared to the scene, sirens blaring, their hoses extinguishing the flames.

Thomas J. Latimer leaned against a tree on the muddy bank of the Darlington Stream's wide end. Kinsley and Isaacs had told him of their findings from their exploratory run at the delta, days ago. He mulled their facts over in his mind as he stared into the clear, bubbling water as it traveled over round, dark stones. The babbling noise was like a lullaby. There was peace in the valley, and love in his heart. He was the youngest of the three adventurers that devised an independent study of this river and its secrets. Scientific papers had been filed indicating that there was an unseasonal spurt of random activity that caused a visible but difficult route to travel into the interior, where no one had been before. He wondered how it could be possible that no one had ever witnessed the flow of this mysterious vein of river water when it mutinied its course and rebelliously sped into an unknown wilderness.

Jason Kinsley and Ivan Isaacs had actually seen it and started to follow it. All of the notes said so. All of the notes were in great detail, until the water forced them to pay attention on how to escape the destiny that lay ahead. They walked through a tangled wall of vines. They wrote that they could see ahead through the foliage, and that the river was still running strong on the other side of the barrier. The passage said, "It appears as though the small rivulet we travel opens out to an enormous lake or gathering place for possibly another river to join this segment of the Darlington."

Tom remembered well why he didn't go with them. He was lovesick over his older woman. She was forty. He was twenty-three, but mature for his age, although emotionally, he was still a baby.

His colleagues were not in favor of his romantic decision to stay with her and help her get settled after the death of her husband. He was the famous Navy pilot, Buck Martin, killed in the crash at the air show. He met her the day her husband was pronounced dead…the day of the show itself. He was one of the volunteers who located the body or parts of it in the flaming wreckage. She had not attended the show. He and a police officer went to her home and notified her of the bad news. She didn't seem too upset in his estimation, but it could have been shock. He was knocked out by her incredible good looks. Being young and healthy, he immediately set his eyes on her for his future. She was medium height with fawn-colored hair and pale blue eyes. Her skin was smooth and inviting. Her lips formed a bow and were painted mauve, with a sheen. Her eyes trained on his. She took in a deep breath when the police sergeant told her that her husband was dead. Her eyes didn't blink. Her gaze remained trained. Was she on drugs, he wondered? Did she not hear the man give her the news? After what seemed a long time, she lowered her eyes and shed a few tears. She looked up, her eyes moist.

"Where is the body?" She asked, as if it were someone else they were talking about. She seemed well-spoken, and her voice was soft, almost musical to his ears. He didn't even know why he was there, in her living room, except that he was the one that found him.

"Unfortunately," began the policeman, "we don't have all the parts of him, yet. We are still looking for one arm." It was then that she paled and looked faint.

Tom put his arm around her to brace her. He looked at the cop and frowned. "I believe you have told her enough, Officer." He led her to the couch. She was light in his arms. He would protect this woman. He could tell that she was intended to be in his life somehow. She wasn't outwardly grieving her husband's death, and she was free for him to pursue her now.

The officer said, as he turned to leave, "I am so sorry I had to give you this news, Mrs. Martin. Your husband was an exceptional man. We will call you when we have his body ready for identification."

He put on his cap as he stepped over the threshold to the outside, beckoning for Tom to follow him. Tom was intensely aroused by this woman who was sending out signals of her own that she sensed a future with him, even though his years were less than hers. He touched her hand as he said, "I will check back to see if you are all right, later." He raised his eyebrows in anticipation of her introducing herself.

She said, "My name is Nara." She smiled weakly and laid back on the couch as she watched him walk to the door. "Thank you."

He noticed that she didn't say, "Nara Martin." That fast, she was a singular person, not attached to her famous fly boy anymore, as though she might be glad that he were out of her life. His imagination led the way.

"I am Tom Latimer, independent water studies. I will be in touch, like I said." Something held their eyes locked for a few moments. He shut the door behind him, bewildered, and walked after the sergeant, who was already getting into the squad car.

Tom had studied the nature of the world's waterways and was important to Isaacs and Kinsley. They had their own expertise and were the providers of the equipment. Tom's financial picture was non-existent, but he was lucky in becoming acquainted with these two men. Things just fell his way. He was not a religious man, but determined to go forward in life and not to dwell on the past. He had everything he wanted. Now, a dazzling and intriguing mate was placed before him. It was Kismet. "Nara," he whispered to himself as the sergeant drove. He smiled.

"What did you say?" asked the policeman, turning his head towards him.

"Nothing. I was thinking out loud."

The sergeant dropped him off at his modest dwelling on the edge of a rural community. It was a single, one story, poorly-built money-maker for some poverty-level, but smart guy who knew that people like Tom existed; people who went cheap to stay alive and have money for more important things...like post-adolescent adventure and exploring. He was a free spirit, no doubt. Already, he was mentally including this new woman in the next excursion with his friends.

Chapter 2

A Bigger Boat

Jase called Tom, who had just returned from his visit to the pilot's widow.

"Hello, Tommy boy. It's Jase. I'm out of the hospital. Isaac is still in traction, and he is still recuperating from the concussion. He will be okay. I talked to him before leaving. The bastard is already game for another journey into the unknown. We both want you along this time. Maybe if you had come with us the first time we would have been successful, and without injury. I'm trying to line up a new boat with all the do-dads we need to find the hidden mouth of the wilderness tributary."

"Glad to hear you're both okay. Yeah, I will be joining you, but I want to bring Nara along…"

"What? Not that dame you met at the air show. Why would you…"

"Hold on, hold on. She can help us. She has offered to fund the expedition, if she can go along. She is interested in the water samples we find in the new channel, if we can find it. She says she knows about it and has even seen it on a kayak trip she took last year.

"Why did you have to include her on this? This is our private investigation. Just because you're stuck on that old broad, we have to suffer? Are you out of your mind?"

"It's my way or else, Jason. She's the love of my life. She comes with us, or I sit this one out again. Good luck. Run it by Ivan, will you? When he is ready to go, we will have a meeting at her house. She's got a real cool spread out in the desert. It's a sprawling rancher with a landing field on the premises. Buck's collection of old airplanes are housed in a huge hangar. She's inherited a fortune. We need her, Jase. It's not just because we are in love that I want her along."

"I'll talk to Ivan and get back to you, but this is really putting a damper on our plans. I don't like taking a woman along on this treacherous trip. I know what happened to us. We have to be so careful. Crossing into that sylvan lake is a precarious undertaking. I am hoping that a bigger boat with sounding devices can get us there. Let's think things through, and I will get back to you. Meanwhile, I want you to really think hard about falling for this cougar. She's just lost her husband, and already she's got you under her spell."

"Wait till you meet her before making a judgment. You will be envious, I guarantee. She's one of a kind."

"See you." Jason hung up, shaking his head, grimacing. "This is awful," he said out loud as he picked up the phone to call Ivan. His white freckled finger pushed the buttons on the phone. His hair was dark red, going gray. His white face had a fading tan, and his eyes were hazel. His eyebrows formed a scowl when he talked to Ivan.

"How are you doing today, pal? Good, good. Hey, I've got some news for you. You're never going to believe what that runt proposes we do..."

Chapter 3

Nara's Place

An air-conditioned paradise is where Nara lived, alone now, on the hot sands of the desert. A wall of purple mountains rose behind the house. She had servants as well as a young Mexican boy to maintain the aqua pool.

Inside, Nara paced in front of the large front window. She was wearing tights and a filmy printed shirt blouse. Her blond hair was loose, in curls around her face. Every now and then she would stoop down to better see the driveway that was blinding to look at because of its white reflective stones. She wore a bracelet of carved bones that looked like ivory.

Carlos, her handyman, had left early, at her dismissal. She was having company of the best kind...a prospective lover, Thomas Latimer, young stud to her liking. How easy it was to lure him into her world and into his dream of finding the wild, evasive branch of the Darlington.

The lavish living room was furnished with a white and beige striped sofa, chairs, and rug. Indian artifacts hung on the walls, and a Buffalo head hung over the six foot fireplace. Tom noticed that there were no photographs of Buck or the two of them together and no pictures of children, pets, or airplanes. It was as though she had lived alone. Maybe they had been separated long before his tragic death. Her lack of grieving should have bothered him, but it didn't. She was all he wanted. It was his fate to nurture this relationship, and see it to the end, 'til death do ye part.'"

Tom rode up the driveway in a cloud of dust in his old El Camino. The paint had faded. It was bright blue when it was new, ions ago. Now, it was used for hauling and getting around as best it could with the help of a local mechanic in town. Parched Prairie was more of an outpost than a vital community. Only those wanting to get away from life dragged their belongings there to live a hard, but uninterrupted life. Ivan and Jase happened to be passing by one day when they met Thomas at the saloon. He recalled their initial conversation.

"I know we can get to it from here," he overheard Jase tell Ivan. They were drinking heavily. Their SUV was cooked, and Tom's mechanic was trying to figure out what was wrong. It was a new vehicle with all of those computerized gadgets…stuff that Tom's auto 'go-to', Charlie B., didn't know about. He and Ivan were getting to that loose-lipped stage of drinking.

Ivan leaned closer to Jase and said, "Let's just stay here a while and ask around…you know, investigate before we do it."

Jase looked up and called to the bar maid. "Another round, please, Miss." He pursed his lips. "Let's get a room somewhere. Shouldn't be hard to find. The town only has two streets. I saw rooms for rent up the road." He checked his pockets for cash and counted three credit cards. "I wonder if they've heard of credit cards here. This is a really out-of-time place we landed in."

Tom was curious. He sauntered over. "Mind if I join you two? I couldn't help but overhear. You can stay at my place for nothing. What are you looking for? Hardly no one ever visits here for fun." He signaled the waitress for another drink for himself and sat down, not waiting for an answer.

Ivan spoke. "Do you know about the Darlington River? We haven't seen it, but have been told there is a maverick branch that emerges randomly and runs through or near this town."

A wide grin spread over his face. He looked up at the ceiling. God is good, he thought. "It's been my life's dream to follow it, when it shows. No one knows where it goes, when it comes, or what prompts it to forge a new hidden route. I'm game to help you find it, if you want. I actually saw it once, but I was just a kid then."

Jase looked at Ivan, and they nodded to each other. "You've got a deal, son. We have kayaks, but no boat. We have a whole mess of other equipment in the car, but it's at the garage. The man's name is Charlie who is working on it. He says it will be a while before he can figure it out. This is mighty nice of you to help us. It's a sure thing if you want to come along. We do need a boat, though." Jase held up his glass and proposed a toast. The other two joined him. "To the Darlington's wild branch! May we sail into the unknown successfully, together!" The glasses clicked, and the men downed their drinks.

The other patrons were old geezers guzzling the cheapest hard liquor the saloon had to offer. Most were missing teeth and had lost most of their white hair. One was asleep on the table behind them, snoring.

"Jenna, put their drinks on my bill and thanks." Tom, young as he was, treated the two men with respect and generosity. He had found the company he needed to form a team. No one that he knew had ever ventured to explore the Darlington. All of the dynamiting and rearranging the state's border lines since the government redrew the map of the United States, caused a lot of changes in the terrain. The pioneering spirit lived on in the hearts of a few, but only one had the capital to fuel their dreams.

Chapter 4

The Dream Team

N<small>ARA OPENED THE DOOR. T</small>OM was just stepping out of the vehicle. He was wearing dusty pointed-toe cowboy boots made of lizard skin, dusty jeans, a denim shirt, and a white Stetson hat. His belt buckle was a copper etching of a wild bull that he had won at a rodeo in the next town. His permanent limp was from an injury sustained from being tossed by 'Bodacious'. That bull broke bones of all his riders, even killed one. Tom was dead drunk when they opened the stall. He had done it on a bet, but he won anyway. If he was sober, he wouldn't have gotten on the back of the beast at any cost.

He was drenched in perspiration. His face was red from heat exhaustion. There was no air conditioner in the El Camino. The drive was long and tiring from his modest shack on the outskirts of Parched Prairie. He grinned. His white teeth gleamed in the sun, picturing her seductive smile. Here was a woman in the know who knew what she wanted and wasn't afraid to ask. Yahoo!

His sexual experiences were comprised of a few times in an alleyway with a homeless girl, getting nude in the haystack at twelve with his cousin, Annie, who was only eight years old and had nothing good to show him, and the bar girl in the next town over where he won the belt buckle. She was his adoring prize. He didn't even remember her name. Betty Louise?

"Hi, Darlin'," said Nara in a sensuous tone. She reached out and touched him on the shoulder. "Come in, come in. It's real cool in here. I'll get you a cold drink. Beer?"

Tom nodded and removed his hat. He wiped his face with his shirt sleeve. "Wow! This feels great." He stepped in and shut the door behind him. He was about six foot three, a long drink of water.

He looked around. No pictures. There was no evidence of her being the wife of a famous pilot. She came back quickly with a bottle of cold Corona. She was sipping a Mint Julip.

"Sit down. Be comfortable." They sat across from each other with the coffee table between them.

"So, how have you been, Nara? I think of you often." He leaned back to adjust to the angle of the couch.

"I am coping nicely. You see, Buck was never home. I think he had another wife in another state. I didn't even care. There was no love between us after a while. Some people are just not meant to be together. It's a shame it takes years to find that out. I'm sorry he's dead, but I am not really grieving, as I guess you might have noticed." She put her finger in her drink to stir it. The ice swirled.

"I'm still sorry. You are all alone out here. It's quite luxurious, but isn't it lonely? Especially at night. Aren't you afraid?"

She put her drink down on the table and sat back, letting her low-cut blouse open more, exposing a white pearly cleavage. She raised her chin and tossed her hair with a flick of her neck. Her lips were full and glistening. "I'm lonely, but never afraid."

"You are a beautiful woman. You shouldn't be alone. It's such a waste." He swigged his beer twice and set down the empty bottle on the table.

"Come here," she said, patting the seat next to her on her loveseat. She reminded him of one of his teachers in high school...the exotic one that taught Spanish...the one that all the boys wanted to bang.

He obeyed and moved to her side. "Put your hands on my breasts." She moved closer to him, thrusting her chest towards his face. She wore no bra. What he was told to caress were free to be touched, nipples inviting him to play. As he pinched them and kissed them and unbuttoned her blouse, she played with his hair, tousling it and rubbing his temples. She smelled good, like expensive perfume.

They were alone. No one could stop what was about to happen. He was totally free and in love with the widow Martin. Somehow, he knew this would be. Her hips began to undulate as she pushed her body towards him. His hands roamed down her spandex tights. She wore no panties. What he sought rose in a mound of down, under his palm. His fingers wandered into the opening, gentle but insistent. She moaned and lay back on the couch, legs spread, the sight of her breasts stimulated him as his organ swelled and stiffened.

He had some moves of his own that he was inventing along the way. Nature told him to move her to the floor, in front of the fireplace. He got on his knees and pulled her to the ground. She was like putty in his hands. His hot fingers pulled off her tights and tossed them aside. He slid her underneath him on the beige carpet. She had removed her filmy blouse and thrown it to the coffee table. There was no shyness about her. She was a lady in the know, and she was hungry. Um, here it comes, she thought. His hot fingers traced circles on her nether region until it screamed for entry. He was a ramrod, a real bucking bronco. She let out a howl he never expected. Damn, he was good, he thought. Damn, he was good, she thought.

They were both panting and spent. She was in a daze, smiling with glazed eyes in the afterglow. "Tommy, I think I love you." She sat up, grabbed her drink and sipped. Her body was still nude before him. He was still aroused. It was so easy to do her, and it was so good. He looked at her before replying.

"I've never told anyone that I loved them before, Nara. I never even thought about it, but I do feel what I think is love for you. And, now…I think this is the way it should feel…overpowering."

She sighed. "Don't go away. I'll get you another." She jumped up and walked to the kitchen. Her buttocks swayed, like two silken melons. Her legs were long and shapely. He we watched her bend over into the bottom of the refrigerator to extract another bottle of beer. What he witnessed gave him another hard-on. He stood up and went into the kitchen, putting his arms around her as she turned. He took the beer and put it on the counter, hands roaming over her curves with his fingers winding up between her legs, feeling for her pleasure spot, finding it, repeating the action in the living room, only this time, standing, with her butt to the wall. She let him do it. She was starved for attention. He was going to be her champion always. He felt like Tarzan. After the second successful launch of his rocket, she all but fell into his strong arms, exhausted and satisfied.

He took his beer and carried her to the couch, placing her gently on the cushions. She reached for her blouse.

"No, not yet. Let me look at you. I don't want this to end."

He stopped her from picking it up.

"This could be a forever thing, you know. Nothing can stop us, Tom." She was full of surprises. She was so easy, and now, she thinks she loves me? She even remembers my name.

He climbed onto the couch, sat down and set her between his legs, his privates a cushion for her soft round posterior. They both drank. The sun caused rippled air waves outside, but they were cool and lost in the joy of pure and natural love-making inside. Her back rested against his chest. Although Tom was game for a third time, he held back, feeling that what was done already was enough for their first encounter. She napped in his arms. He laid his head back and closed his eyes, wondering if she would go with him, Jase, and Ivan on their secret run. As strange as the whole day was, they slept that way until the sun set. The sky was a glorious bright orange, red and pink. The sand reflected the colors, and coyotes howled. Tumbleweeds rolled by outside as the air current changed from red hot to cool.

Nara wakened first, rubbing her eyes and smiling when she remembered what had transpired earlier. He was still there...her captive love slave. It was good to have a warm body in the house. She looked out the window from the couch and slowly eased off his dozing body. As she slid away, he opened one eye and then the other. He was grinning. When he saw her try to sneak away, he pulled her back down.

"Not so fast, young lady. You look good with sunset on your skin." She fell on top of him. He positioned her to 'go again'.

"Let's go to the pool," she said, pulling him up with her. It's nice and warm now. Soon, it will be dark. Come on."

He rose and followed her through the sliding door into the stuffy atmosphere of days' end on the desert. When they reached the edge of the glittering blue pool, Nara dove into the deep end, gracefully gliding to the ladder, climbing to the diving board. She plunged into the pool. Tom dove in to join her. He swam under the water and landed a few feet from her, grabbed her, and they swam together underwater, kissing and embracing. When they came to the surface, they were laughing and doing acrobatics together under the water, under the darkening sky. They engaged in sex one more time, submerged under the surface. Cool air moved over hot sand, making it almost cold, giving their skin goose bumps. Pool lights and other ground lights automatically came on.

Nara pulled herself out of the water onto the cement and walked to the chair where two towels were draped. Her nude body gleamed with droplets in early moonlight. She wrapped herself in one. Tom clung to the side of the pool watching her before joining her on the deck.

They sat together in the dark, huddled in warm terry cloth, the moon and stars lighting up the desert panorama.

Nara asked, "Can you spend the night, Tom?"

"I'd love to, but I have to get back tonight."

He didn't want to say no, but wanted to get back to his house to call Jason. Their big plan to explore the Darlington was in its beginning stages. He was thinking of asking her to go with them, but would wait for a day or so. He knew she would say yes. There was nothing holding her back. He was glad that she didn't have children. He didn't want to have to share her with anyone. He didn't notice the age difference, only that she was more confident than most women and more willing to engage.

Chapter 5

The Day of Departure

Ivan was rolled out the hospital doors to the pavement where Jase and Tom were waiting. He got up and into the car with no problem. His legs had healed, and his head wound had been treated. He waved to the nurse, as they pulled away from the curb.

Tom turned in his seat to talk to Ivan in the back. "So, I'm glad you're out. I am really excited about this trip. I think we're going to do it this time. I feel it. Are you ready to go in a few days?"

"Of course, but Jase tells me that you want to bring that woman along. What's with that? What can she offer that we don't already know or have?"

"Money to fund us. We need a great boat. I'll show it to you and help you make up your mind about Nara. She's wonderful." Tom said, grinning.

Jason commented. "It's true we need the money, but you just met her. Her husband just died. How can you get involved with a grieving widow?"

"It's not like that, Jase. They were separated. She is single now, and she digs me. She also knows about the river. She saw it split when she was kayaking last year. She would have followed it, but she was alone;

thought better of it, not knowing where it was going. So, she is just as curious and game as we are."

"I don't like having a woman on the boat. Folk lore says that it is bad luck," said Ivan, frowning.

"Wait till you guys see the boat. It's docked not far from here."

"How did you find it?" asked Jason.

"She told me about a marina. I looked around and found a charter. It's our dream boat. We won't be tossed out of it on our asses, like you were in that bark." Tom turned back to watch the road. "Let's swing by it on the way back to my place. Take the next left off the highway, and I'll direct you from there. It's called Mercury Boat Sales and Rentals. There's a big sign."

Jase followed Tom's directions, and they parked in the lot of the marina. The noonday sun glinted off the metal roof of the building. He knew right away which craft was the chosen one. It was a beauty…a white yacht named, The Ocean Glory. It rocked gently on the river waves.

Ivan had fallen asleep in the back seat. His head was tilted back, and his arms were at his sides.

"Hey! Isaacs! Wake up and take a look at her. She's our lady of the river, The Ocean Glory." Tom got out of the car and opened the back door.

Jason stretched his legs after shutting the driver's door. He scanned the horizon. "Today would be perfect for our launch."

"It's a CAVU day, as Buck Martin would say, if he were still alive," said Tom, squinting at the horizon.

There were no clouds, just deep blue sky overhead. He imagined a foreign world beyond the sprawling Darlington waterway. So, Nara had seen it. He wondered why she hadn't recorded her findings and written a paper on it to send to scientific interest groups. He guessed she was not into academia. Of course, he wasn't either, but he needed the scholars, Jase and Ivan, to help him in the expedition. Tom only collected water samples for the bio-conscious community and worked hard labor at the cement plant in the next town. His aspiration was in this trip to find the wild branch…he called it, the Darlington Rogue. It excited him and the others to be the first to really break the barrier and sail into the sylvan haven on the other side. With this boat that Nara would supply, it could be done. His body heated up thinking about her. He was 'bewitched, bothered, and bewildered' by her charms.

"Tom! Come here." It was fully out-fitted for adventure of the exploratory kind. Tom got a good feeling, looking at the sleek body of the yacht.

"Well, I don't think we will be in the ocean, but that rogue branch might lead us to a body of water as big as a small ocean. I never heard of a metallic sheen on a silver expanse of water before. Maybe it is from undiscovered or mined minerals."

"Good a guess as mine, Sherlock. We're going to solve this mystery, even though we have to take along our female patron," said Jason.

Ivan slowly walked around to see the name inscribed on the back of the vessel. He grinned. "This is just what the doctor ordered." He felt his seeping head bandage that looked like a skimpy turban. "When do we sail, Captain?" He looked at Jason, as he was the pilot of small river craft.

"I haven't run a boat this big before, but it can't be much different from the ones in the marina. I'm sure we'll have instructions on board along with sonar devices and a marine GPS. Let's board her and have a look."

Jason stepped forward to the planked dock.

"Hey!" shouted the harbor master, running down to the boat. "No trying out rentals. I guarantee this is out of your league. It's our most expensive yacht, and we don't allow anyone on board, unless the money is up front."

"What a jerk!" said Tom, turning to face the man, who was now standing in front of him. He was a fat, balding, unkempt old man with a pair of dark glasses, so his eyes couldn't be seen. He wore a dirty white khaki shirt and wrinkled pants.

"We are going to rent this boat, man," said Jason, walking up to him, keeping his calm.

"Well, now that's different. I will need money either for deposit or full rental." He stuck out his hand to Jason and said his name was Fermin Levine. Jason shook it and cocked his head.

Tom said, "We want to buy her, not rent her." He gave a crooked smile at Levine and waited for his reaction.

"You couldn't have enough to purchase her. She's a fine yacht with quite a history. She was used in marine salvage missions. She has papers, like a pedigreed dog."

Tom wrote a check for a deposit to hold her until he had a chance to talk to Nara. He didn't foresee any problems with financing The Ocean Glory. He thrust it at Levine. Levine snatched it and studied it, taking off his glasses, as though he could see better with more light.

"That's more than I would have asked to hold her. When do you want to take her? And what do you want with a boat like this?" he asked.

Ivan said, "You don't need to know that, Mr. Levine. Your job is to sell boats to keep your shabby marina going. It would be wise to not play interrogator." He looked him dead in the eye, with a threatening stare.

Levine didn't comment, but asked, "When will you be back? I have to know, so that I can give you the keys. I have to be here, and I want these checks to clear before you take off for parts unknown." He put his glasses back on and glowered back at them.

"Give us a week. I'll be in touch with you. The money is good, believe me." Tom signaled for them to get back into the car. They drove off to Tom's house.

The shabby little cottage rose out of a crop of pale, wild weeds. Some roofing shingles lay about on the ground. It was clearly an uncared-for rental. It was good enough to house the three river rats that longed to reach 'Nirvana'."

After settling in the small living room, Tom called Nara to tell her what they had in mind. He walked into the kitchen for privacy. Ivan lay down on the sagging couch to rest, holding his head. Jason asked him if he had any pills to take.

"In my shirt pocket there is a bottle of pain-killers with an anti-inflammatory effect. Can you reach in and get me one with a glass of water, please. I just need to rest a while."

"Sure." He retrieved the bottle of pills and headed for the kitchen. He overheard Tom say, "Sure, sure. I know. I will be over in a little while to help you with that."

With what? Jase wondered. Most likely, Tom didn't have this plan sewed up yet, but he left it to his sexual prowess to seal the deal. He and Jase would just chill and go over inventories for supplies when Ivan woke from his nap.

"Do you want me to go to Nara's place with you, Tom?" "No. No, that isn't a good idea. Leave this up to me. It's as good as done." The conversation with Nara was over. There were plans to have dinner at her house. She lived a ways from him in the desert. He was excited about everything that was happening in his life. Tom never considered failure an option.

Tom's car threatened to overheat as he arrived close enough to see her house. The pool was glittering like a blue diamond in the sun. As he sputtered over the last half mile, he wondered if she would let him see the planes in the hangars. He wished her husband was alive so that he could hear him tell his aviation stories. Why on earth did he leave her for another woman? Nara was rare. She was super-intelligent and uncommonly beautiful.

He finally reached the turn-around in front of the house and parked the car. The smell of seafood wafted out from the house. It was not something experienced in this 'neck of the woods'. There were no desert clams that he knew of, nor lobster. He had only had shrimp once in Waco when he went to his aunt's funeral. She was his last living relative. Those in attendance were only two of her closest friends, a couple up in years. They asked him out to dinner with the money she left them and prodded him into trying shellfish. He liked it, but would more than likely not eat it again, at least fresh, in Parchment Prairie.

Wiping the sweat off his forehead with his shirt-sleeve, he took off his Stetson, walked up to the door, and knocked.

"I'll be right there," came her sexy, mature woman's voice. She enunciated very clearly. He stood, dripping with perspiration, longing to take a dip in her glorious pool. The door opened after a few minutes. She appeared. To his express shock, his eyes beheld her nude body, glistening with some kind of perfumed oil. "Come in. I hope you are hungry. I have prepared a fresh feast from the sea."

He walked into the cool interior of her home. The air conditioner was set for freezing. She took his hat and threw it onto the couch. He stood quite still, letting her do as she would with him, noticing all of the pink shrimp and white scallops and whole lobsters on the dining room table.

She tussled with his belt buckle and undid his pants. No underwear. This was good. It made it easier for her to seduce him. She pulled them to his ankles, and he kicked them off into a corner of the room. She carefully unbuttoned his white cotton shirt that was wet with sweat. She tossed it onto the couch.

"There. Just look at you, you handsome cowboy, you. Save the ride for after we eat. Then, we can swim for a while until the sun goes down. Sound good?"

What choice did he have? He wanted her, and he wanted the boat. It was a pleasurable bargain for him. She told him she had so much money from Buck's estate that she didn't know how to spend it all. He would supply her with his wish list after the evening got underway.

"Yee-hah, woman!" He grabbed her tightly and she slipped out of his arms with her oiled skin. "There are so many good smells here. I want to eat them all."

She took his hand, and they were seated before the sliding glass door that looked out on the sand and the mountains behind. There were trays of every kind of seafood...oysters, mussels, and crab.

"Where did you get all this stuff? It's unheard of to have these items even on menus at restaurants here." He forked some shrimp onto his plate. There were no side dishes, like coleslaw or potatoes.

She watched him greedily bite into each morsel.

"I have them imported from Texas and California and freeze them in the freezer in my pantry. They are frozen, but they are fresh and untreated with preservatives or fillers.

He didn't realize how hungry he was and wondered how Jase and Ivan would enjoy the canned beans and bacon he had in his larder. They would enjoy the beer, though; speaking of which, Nara reached into a cooler on the floor and pulled out two cold beer bottles. He was in heaven.

He watched her eat. As she did so, her voice uttered a little almost inaudible sound like, "mmm". It wasn't cute, but he guessed, that was her way. There were shells everywhere. He found it strange that there were no dipping sauces. In Waco, there was a dish of horseradish and ketchup mixed together that they put on the shrimp. It was called cocktail sauce. Where was she from? He didn't know much about her. Did it matter? His history wasn't very interesting. He was glad that she didn't ask him questions about his past or what he did for a living.

There was no music. The only sound was of them cracking shells, which she did with her teeth, and the air conditioner humming. It was very bright in the dining room, even though the walls were painted deep blue. Every now and then, his eyes would catch sight of her plump fleshy breasts with their pink raised nips when they rested on the table in front of her plate.

Once his appetite for food abated, his thoughts turned to her naked body and the slippery, scented skin. He had never been in her bedroom. It must be like a palace, he thought. She knew quality and how to enjoy it.

He wasn't self-conscious in front of her when he stood up. She had reassured him that he not only had a gorgeous male body, but was the best lover she had ever had. She told him that Buck had a small one and was short, besides. He was a courageous fly-boy, but the water was her element.

She had the smell of oysters on her breath when he kissed her. There were even particles of seafood between her small teeth. He didn't really care. It occurred to him that some of that catch would be tainted, but he put that thought aside, feeling just stuffed, not poisoned. There was something strange about her and the situation. He decided to focus on the trip and the exciting discovery of the rogue branch's destination…and the silver lake, what Jason and Ivan swore they experienced before the accident in the bark.

Chapter 6

Ready to Go

Tom drove home after he and Nara made love in her bed and in the pool. She tried to get him to stay underwater with her, but his lungs were about to burst, and he had to surface. She stayed under a long time, making circles in the water and swimming underwater laps. Finally, she surfaced with no evidence that she had held her breath for such a long time. He was amazed at her stamina.

"What are you, a mermaid?" He helped her out.

They both sat on the side of the pool.

"I'm sorry, I forgot that you..." She stopped abruptly.

"That I what? Have normal human being lung capacity?" He laughed. "Come on, what's your secret? Were you a swimming champion at one time?"

"Yes, I was. I have extraordinary lung capacity from practicing all the time when I was on the high school and college swim teams. We had deep diving competitions. I won them all."

Tom stared at her, his mind going a mile a minute. Her ability was uncanny.

"Where were you born and raised? Around here?" He stood up and helped her to her feet. The pre-sunset breeze blew her hair around. It was almost platinum in the golden rays. Her skin had a sheen.

She put her head down. "I grew up in Florida with my father. He was a scientist involved in marine biology. He was noted in Geographic circles. She stared off into the mountains and continued with her story. He's dead now. I met Buck at an air show in Daytona Beach. We hit it off right away. I was impressed with his skills and his nerve as a Navy pilot. He was much in demand by aviation agencies. He had flown rescue missions for marine explorers. My father had employed him to handle his last expedition. He built this house in the desert, so that we could preserve our privacy and enjoy the luxuries money could buy."

Tom listened carefully, trying to put the clues together. So far, they made sense.

"What about you? Are you a prairie native?" She reached for a towel from the lounge chair.

"Don't cover up just yet. I like watching your body." He smiled.

"Well, how about you?" she persisted.

"I was born in Texas. I was raised with my old maid aunt. I'm afraid my mother didn't want me. I never knew her. She was young, single, and headed for an early death due to drug abuse. I guess I should be glad that I had some place to go, but that was then, and now is now. I took off when I was eighteen to get away from Texas. I didn't like the climate, and I hate scorpions."

"But, there are scorpions here, too. It's just as hot and dry."

"Yes, but there's very little rain...no floods. Besides, I met my two adventuring buddies here in the saloon. They were fleeing their empty lives, too, with a dream to find the rogue offshoot."

She listened and nodded. "Do you have a good boat and equipment?"

He laughed. "No. My friends used a bark to get through the mystery entrance when the river branched last time. They sustained injuries and are lucky to be alive, actually. I didn't go with them. I had other things to think about, but now...I want you to join us. I think you would be a great addition to our crew."

"Listen, I will fund the trip and go with you. Pick the biggest boat in the marina and let me know who to make out the check to and how much it will cost."

"Really? You would do that for us?" He thought she would offer, but it was so easy.

"For the cause, for the chance to discover an undiscovered phenomenon." Her eyes were bright and full of courageous desire to get started.

He kissed her and threw a white towel over her shoulders. It was getting chilly. Their skin bore goose-bumps.

"I can't wait!" He couldn't stop kissing her. They made love on the hot cement around the pool.

"Come into the house. Let's get dressed and have a drink. I'm going to write you a blank check, so that you can have it for tomorrow. Let's waste no time. The river might be about to split soon. I know it's a random happening, but the moon seems to be in the right position to coax things. I have studied it on my own."

"You are too much. Why on earth did that crazy guy ever leave you?"

Sitting at the dining room table with the leftovers and the wine, they toasted to the beginning of a journey into the unknown.

Not wanting to leave too abruptly, he excused himself, saying that he needed his rest for the upcoming trip, and he had to get back to the others.

He lingered at the doorway, putting on his Stetson, his form silhouetted against the desert night sky. He said, "I want you to meet Ivan and Jase. You will like them. They are great companions. I know they will love you, too. Who couldn't?"

"Fine. Get going. I am tired, too. Talk to you tomorrow." She planted a warm, long kiss on his lips before he got into his truck. The engine was cool now, making his ride home more enjoyable...no sputtering, just the rumble of his old engine.

Ivan and Jason were cooking their dinner when he walked into his house. The air smelled of bacon and beans. They had found the beer and were drinking heartily. Their plates rested on the coffee table. They were watching the news. The weatherman joked about the emergence of a wild branch of the Darlington due to manifest soon. "Of course, it's only a rumor, something we news people love to spread and keep alive. I don't think I would be going to look for it. It's only a mirage."

"Oh, yeah?" retorted Ivan. "We will see about that. I can see us on the news after we bring back pictures and samples from the sylvan lake."

"I will be the photo-journalist. I've already documented your trip from what you told me, Jase." He brought out the journal that held the photos and copy. "Relive your adventure. It's all here. Everything you gave me, I put in order. Look! Look!" He swallowed his beer and belched. He couldn't stop smiling. "And, look at this!" He pulled out the blank check from his shirt pocket. "That boat is ours tomorrow."

"You lucky bastard!" Jase snatched the check from his hand while Ivan turned the pages of the travelogue. "Sweet Jesus! It's blank. We can cash it at the bank and have more than enough to buy supplies as well as the boat."

"You're going to meet with her before we embark. Let's buy the boat and then go to her house to discuss our plans and have some drinks. I'm sure she will let you use the pool, too. She's got a sweet setup. And, by the way, she's mine." He grinned. "Wait till you see her. I told you she saw the rogue from her kayak, but couldn't follow it because she was alone. She is psyched." He downed another beer.

"We need supplies. You have nothing to take with us in the form of food. We're going to need a lot of prepackaged meals and dried fruit," said Jason.

"Don't forget plenty of bottled water and some Vodka…a case should do." Ivan said as he picked up the paper plates and dumped them in the trash can. "Maybe a case of Jack Daniels for you Irish guys."

"What we don't want is to get drunk. We need our wits about us. It's kind of mysterious that we can see the river break off into its own path into the wilds, but no one has reported observing it at the other end where and if it empties."

"We'll find out, Tom. Get your girlfriend over here for a meeting. I don't think we should waste time traveling to her house. This is serious business, and time is of the essence." Jason stood up to his full height of six-foot-four and stretched.

"I'll call her now." Tom went into the bedroom for privacy. He didn't know if she would go for the idea of driving over to his place for this meeting, but she agreed to meet with them the next morning. She had her equipment organized and would pack her vehicle that night.

"I miss you, lady," he said to her before hanging up. She didn't respond, but hung up, softly. It slightly disturbed him that she wasn't in lover mode, but maybe he should cool it, anyway. She was becoming a habit with him.

The next morning as Tom, Ivan, and Jason prepared breakfast, Nara's car pulled up in front of the house. They fought to see her through the front window.

"What's with you two?" Tom said, pushing them away. I told you, behave yourselves. She's mine." He hoped she was wearing clothes. She was kind of an exhibitionist.

The men laid silverware on the table and put out basic dishes. Ivan tended to the coffee.

"Wait until she comes in before cooking anything. I don't know what she likes. I know she's mad for seafood, but we don't have any of that."

The men waited in line for her to come to the door. She left her gear in the vehicle and got out. She wore short shorts, a halter top that squeezed her ample breasts together and created a huge cleavage, and had sandals on her feet. Ivan and Jason were all but drooling over her. Tom was proud that he had landed her and her money.

He opened the door and ushered her into the dark, shabby interior of his home.

Ivan stepped forward extending his hand. "I am Ivan Isaacs, marine specialist." He smiled as he fondled her small white hand. Tom elbowed him. He backed away and let Jason step forward.

"My pleasure. I am Nara, daughter of Professor Horace Nordic. He worked closely with Dr. Warren Wild, author of "The Reversal of Darwin's Theory: Proof of Man's Aquatic Superiority'."

"I am Jason Kinsley, mastermind of all things impossible; hence the quest of the rogue branch on the Darlington." He bowed forward, took her hand and kissed it.

Tom nudged him away, too. "These are my two scraggly, but lovable cohorts. Keep your distance. Neither has been this close to a woman for a long time." He laughed and poked Ivan in the shoulder.

Ivan said, "I hear you have seen the rogue. Do you know where it comes into the river? I think it will be visible with the position of the moon. At least, that's what I read on the Internet."

"Yes. I believe it will stay active for a week. We are right on time. Gentlemen, I would like a cup of coffee."

"Of course. How rude of us. Have a seat and thank you for all of your help. The Ocean Glory is the boat we need. You have made it all possible." Jason pulled out a chair.

"That boat used to belong to Dr. Wild, but it was willed to my father when Wild died. It was sold when my father died and wound up at the Mercury Marina."

Ivan poured the coffee. Tom placed a kiss on her cheek to lay claim to his prize in front of his friends. She took his hand and rubbed it against her cheek. Although youthful and beautiful, she was old enough to be his mother.

"Uh, we're so glad you are coming with us," said Ivan, lying through his teeth. He saw trouble already with the hanky-panky issue at hand. Tom was a baby. This was his sexy mama. They didn't need this distraction on such an important mission.

"Thank you. It is also my dream to travel these wild waters and see where it all leads. I also thought that if we do find life or a veritable Valhalla, we might have to stay there if it closes over, until the next appearance." She picked up a biscuit and buttered it.

She was comfortable with these men, having some kind of insight that they did not possess. Her perfume permeated the room, sweetening the smell of unclean things in the house.

Two vehicles arrived at the marina in River Bend. Levine was expecting them. He came out of his little office, chewing on a cigar, dark glasses reflecting the sun, his flip-flops slapping against the pebbled driveway. He was smiling. Nara paid a handsome price to get The Ocean Glory. He checked out her financial report and found that she was loaded.

Jason and Tom parked their vehicles behind the office to stay there until they returned. Levine was going to charge them a fee for parking, but included it in the boat fee.

They began loading the boat with their gear. Nara walked up to Levine and spoke to him. He pointed to the entranceway of the marina at a truck that was heading toward the slip where The Ocean Glory was docked. She nodded and went back to the boat. The truck backed up and opened the rear door. There were barrels of seafood to be unloaded. The items were packed in ice and sealed. These barrels were going to be loaded below decks in the refrigerated area.

Jason and Ivan were surprised. Tom said, "Hey, she likes shellfish. It is pure protein, you know. Lighten up. It's not just for her. We can eat it, too. I think it is very generous of her."

"She must dig you, Thomas. You are a lucky man," said Jason. He watched Nara instruct the delivery man to the hull of the ship with the barrels.

"Okay, let's finalize the vehicle security before we go." Ivan walked toward Levine, squinting at the sun.

That magic moment of readiness occurred. They stood on the deck, Jason at the helm. The sun was strong for early morning. A few white puffy clouds drifted in the sky. Jason started the engine, after opening the hatch to warm it up. It sounded like thunder. The craft rocked side to side. Tom had his arm around Nara's small waist. She put on her sun glasses and looked up at him.

"Thank you for making my dream come true. I am so excited about discovering where the rogue leads."

"You have made my dream and that of Jason and Ivan come true, too. Without you, we could not do this."

He leaned down and kissed her. She returned his kiss then, braced herself by grasping the railing as The Ocean Glory pulled away from the dock.

Ivan busied himself checking the ropes and the safety jackets below decks. He jumped up the steps to the top deck and stood beside Jason. "I've got the maps. When you get into open water, go north on the river. Nara said that's where she witnessed the rogue."

Jason nodded. The boat was a dream. It was sleek, it was powerful, and it was loaded with state of the art equipment.

Jason steered the craft out of the marina bay and headed north. The breeze blew their hair, and the sun tanned their skin. The water was blue and wide with luscious green plants and trees on the banks.

Nara finished drinking her coffee and smiled into the breeze, eyes shut in contentment.

Tom had his arm around her. "Do you think we are on time? Think we'll see it soon?"

She nodded, grinning. "I know we will find it and be able to get through. I just know it."

He decided to believe in her certainty, wondering underneath it all why she was so sure. Love conquers all, and he believed he was in love. His friends chose to believe in her abilities to maintain positivity, too.

"I'll show you where I used to swim when we are adrift." She took his arm and led him below decks to a large room with a huge glass tank filled with water. The water vibrated with the noise of the engine.

"An indoor swimming pool. Cool." He walked up to the glass and puts his palms on it. "It feels cold. Too cold for me. Would you swim in there?"

"Sure. I like cold water. Maybe later, when we have had all the sun we can take, we can cool off in here. It's dark and private. I don't want the others to use it. It's just for us."

"Why not?"

"It's my boat and my money. I have my own rules, okay? You and I have something going here. They are not a part of that, right?"

He slowly answered, "Yes, you are right. I'll tell them."

"Good," she said.

"What are all of these barrels doing here?"

"Don't worry. This is all of the oysters and other types of raw seafood I had brought on board. Each barrel is packed with ice, and there is a cooling line that is attached to each barrel to keep them frozen. We can rendezvous in here and have a midnight snack in the water. What do you think?"

He heaved a sigh. "I guess it could be fun."

She cocked her head. "In case you are afraid you will get me pregnant, I didn't have children, because I can't. We can be natural with each other. I think I'm falling in love with you, Tommy."

She leaned into him. Her skin was cool and pearl-white. She was confident in her approach to his heart. Was it because she was older... the cougar? Or, was he inexperienced, immature, and naïve?

"Sounds good to me...very good." He put her hand on his throbbing male appendage and said, "I could go for a cold swim now. How about it?"

She pulled off her clothing and started up the ladder. He couldn't take his eyes off her perfect derriere as each hip moved her to the lip of the tank.

As he began to unbutton his shirt and trip out of his pants, a voice called out, "Where are you Tom? Where is Nara? Are you two together?" He knocked on the door and opened it, finding Tom naked and Nara swimming nude in the tank.

Tom was shocked and embarrassed. He looked at Nara, who was unaffected by Ivan's presence in the room. She kept swimming in circles and touching the bottom of the tank, and zooming to the top. She didn't seem to need air.

"Ivan! Listen, I have to talk to you about this."

He began to put his clothes on, covering his naked butt and frontal view. He turned his back to the tank.

Ivan said, "Look, you can't be messing around while Jason and I plot our course to the rogue. At least put in some time before fooling around." He lustily eyed Nara who seemed to be enjoying being watched. She didn't come out to help defend herself and Tom. She held the cards. "It looks like a great place to cool off and keep fit."

Nara came to the glass and frowned at Tom. Her breasts were pressed against the glass.

"Nara doesn't want you or Jason to have access to the tank. It's her boat and her rules. I told her I would let you know." When dressed, he tried to usher Ivan out of the room and back up onto the deck. He reluctantly walked into the hallway with Tom behind him. He turned back to Nara and shrugged. "Have a nice swim. I'll see you later, topside."

She waved and blew bubbles at him, jumping out of the water like a fish and diving back down to the bottom. He shut the door and went up the steps to the main the deck.

Nara splashed around some more and came out of the tank to open one of the barrels of seafood. She pried the lid off with a tire iron. Inside were raw oysters, glistening in a sea of crystal ice chips. The second layer contained crabs and mussels. She began to drool. It was time to feed.

Tom joined Jason and Ivan at the helm as The Ocean Glory sped down the wide river. The Darlington was a new river, being created by the EPA during the re-assigning of state's boundaries. A beaver dam kept the water diverted. The experiment was a success. But, no matter how many fish they stocked, they didn't prosper and repopulate like the natural rivers in that area or across the nation. The boat purred and spat out bilge water when Jason slowed it down. They decided to idle and get their bearings. An hour had passed since they left the marina.

"Where is Nara?" asked Jason.

"She's getting cooled off below decks. There is a huge tank of cold water and a shitload of barreled fresh shellfish that is iced by a coolant system. I told you she adores seafood. It is her boat, after all. That is her private territory, aside from her cabin for sleeping. She wants you guys to respect her request to stay away from the tank."

"Geez, that's weird. You sure can pick 'em, young-blood," said Jase.

Ivan lectured him. "I didn't mean to break in on you, but I really didn't think anything funny would be going on. This is a serious mission, and we are not even half way there. We need her to guide us to where she found the entrance to the rogue waterway. And, by the way, you lucky dog, she has one hot bod for an older woman."

"That's enough out of you. Don't talk about her like that. I'll go..." Tom heard the hatch open and watched Nara, now clothed in halter top and cut-offs, approach them. Her pale hair was wet and clung to her shoulders.

She put on her sunglasses and put her arm around Tom's waist. "What's going on? How far have we come, and why are we idling in the middle of the Darlington? Shouldn't we be making headway toward the rogue?"

Ivan and Jason trained their eyes on her. Tom gave her a squeeze and held her against him while the boat idled, sputtering and making little waves that slapped against its sides.

Tom began, "We need you to help us locate the opening where the rogue begins. You said…"

Ivan reprimanded her, subtly. "We thought you two were in on our adventure. Then, you disappeared. Jason and I have been scanning the banks for a clue where we can divert. Are you on this journey for serious purpose or just a wild ride?"

Nara kept her cool. Tom snapped back in her defense. "Lay off, Ivan. This is technically Nara's yacht. Without her, we would not be here. And, if she wants to go below decks, it's her business."

Jason turned away from the wheel and added, "I think you should apologize to Nara, Ivan. We've just begun our search. She's with us now, so let's start over with a new attitude, all right?"

Nara responded. "I understand. We are all excited. I will be more attentive, gentlemen. This is new to me. I want to be of value to you. Let me see the map."

Ivan handed it to her. She took it to a table to spread it out and weighted down the corners. There was a breeze blowing over the water, rumpling the paper. An open laptop held the same configuration. She magnified it. They weren't close to the opening yet, if indeed, it were there. According to her calculations, though, it would be, and it would be accessible to the great beyond.

She traced the river with her finger and studied the indications of a switch-off where the rogue began.

"I was kayaking in the direction we are traveling. Only, it was up farther where I entered the water. The pier that rents them was in a town called, Stony Run. The beach is all pebble. The current is swift there. I will know it when we come upon it. If it's still there, there will be a U-shaped tree branch of enormous proportion leaning out from the bank."

"How far is it from here, do you think; and, how long will it take us to get there? Are we talking hours or days?" Jason was the most curious. He was the captain.

"I can't be sure, but I don't think it will take more than a day, maybe not as long. We might be able to fulfill our dream today before dark. I wouldn't want to go beyond the light of the sun to explore."

Jason started up the powerful engine, and the four explorers held on as the boat lurched forward. Nara put the map aside and joined the others, using binoculars to scout out the banks and jutting boulders that might be in their way.

Tom pointed to something sticking out that was white, like a molded point, not like rock. "What is that? I've never seen anything like that before in the river. It looks like a piece of bleached dinosaur bone."

All eyes turned to the object near the bank. "Maybe it is a dinosaur bone. No one travels this river. Maybe all of the upheaval of the government turning the landscape into different territories and eliminating mountain ranges has something to do with it, like stirring up old corpses in a flooded graveyard," said Jason.

Ivan took a look through his binoculars. They were passing it. "Let's steer over there and have a closer look. I am curious. Let's take a sample of it with us."

Nara was silent. Tom thought he caught her smiling. There was nothing funny about what they were witnessing.

"What do you think it is, Nara?"

"I think it is most likely some kind of rock, like calcified lime. It is a form of sedimentary rock. Unusual, but new things are cropping up everywhere in everything, every year now. We are witnessing the evolution of Earth. I say we just keep going. We've got several hours to go before the rogue reveals itself."

"She's right, Ivan. I'm staying on course. Hey, can someone bring me a sandwich and a drink. I need plenty of ice in it. Maybe you can take over the helm, Latimer."

Nara responded. "I will bring up a tray from the kitchen for us all. We can eat in the shade on deck."

Tom took over the wheel, and Nara went below to get lunch.

Ivan stood next to him, still eying the surroundings. "It was a good idea to bring her, Tom. She knows her place, serving us men. She's all right in my book." He winked.

"It's no wonder you are single, if that's all you think of women," Tom returned.

The sharp point of the white rock or whatever it was dimmed to a speck behind them in their wake. The sun was directly overhead. The breeze on the water smelled of plant life and honeysuckle. They spotted herons on the bank.

As they glided along, Tom cut the engine. The boat rocked. Nara appeared with a tray of sandwiches and iced tea. Her pale skin was looking dry.

"Let me put some lotion on you," said Jason, reaching for the hot plastic bottle of sun screen.

She let him rub the oil all over her exposed skin. She closed her eyes and rolled her shoulders.

"Thank you. I forgot how hot and dry the air can be on the water. I'd rather be under the water."

He stopped applying the lotion. They ate. Four hours on the river and they weren't there yet. Perhaps around the bend it would manifest.

As they ate, Tom reminded them that the moon would be full that night, and that even if they located the branch of the rogue, they should wait until morning to explore it.

"You are right," said Nara. "It was a full moon the night before I saw the mysterious cut off to the unknown waterway. Besides, we need time to unwind and gear up for the trip. We should all be on board with the map and our duties."

"I'm glad you're sailing with us, Nara. You are a valuable addition to our crew." Jason wiped his mouth and set down his napkin. It blew off into the water.

"Thank you for preparing lunch for us. It was an unexpected luxury to be served," said Ivan, noticing how Nara's skin was beginning to wrinkle in the sun.

"I am taking a swim to cool off. Anyone want to join me?" she asked.

Tom said, "I don't think it's a good idea. You don't know how deep this river is or how strong is the current."

"I told you I was on the diving team in high school. I am very comfortable in the water. I can even scout out what's on the bottom. I was a champion diver."

She left the table and went below, returning completely nude, her white body beginning to wrinkle from lack of hydration. She walked past them. They ogled her, much to Tom's dismay. He was shocked that she didn't care who saw her body, beautiful as it was.

Before he could say anything to her, she dove off the side of the boat and disappeared in the dark water.

"She doesn't have any breathing apparatus to be diving," said Jason, standing up, looking over the rail into the smooth water.

"She has no inhibitions, that's for sure," said Ivan, joining Jase and Tom at the rail.

"I want her to be safe," said Tom.

"Should we look for her? She hasn't come up to breathe!" Jason was worried.

Tom knew that she could handle herself, but didn't like the ruckus she was creating among his friends.

A long time passed, and she didn't surface.

"I feel like we are witnessing a drowning. We should do something. Tom, she's your woman…aren't you concerned? Don't you think someone should jump in and look for her?"

Fifteen minutes had passed, and before any of them made an attempt to rescue Nara, her head popped up in the middle of the river. She didn't even gasp after holding her breath so long. She was smiling and waving to them.

"She was right. She is a champion. I don't know of anyone that could have done what she did," said Jason.

"Come back to the boat!" shouted Tom. "We have to push on. It's getting late."

She nodded her shiny head and swam on the surface to the side of the boat. Tom pulled her up. The men turned their heads, reluctantly. Her body was pearl white and smooth as porcelain. She needed that swim.

Tom led her below decks to get clothes on. Jason and Ivan exchanged glances. Ivan took over the wheel and started the engine.

In her cabin Nara dried off and put on her shorts and top. Tom sat on the bunk and watched her. He was excited, but now was not the time for frolicking under the covers.

"So," she began, "it is murky under the surface. There are a lot of trees that are still growing. I went all the way to the bottom. It is littered with fish bones. I didn't see anything else aquatic, just waving seagrass and mud."

She pressed her cold body against his. She kissed his lips and ran her fingers through his hair.

He pulled away from her. "You know what you are doing to me?"

"We're bunking together. Later, we can really be together," she answered.

"You could have gotten killed with that stunt. I know you are good, but you didn't know what lurked under the surface. You could have gotten trapped in the wild branches of the trees or...."

"You have to learn to trust me, Thomas. I come from extraordinary stock. Let's get above and lend a hand to the others. We should be approaching the bend now where the river narrows."

Chapter 7

The Entrance to the Rogue

On deck, Jase and Ivan changed positions at the wheel. Ivan asked Jase, "Did you notice anything strange about Nara's body?" He anticipated a yes.

"You mean the lack of a belly-button?" Jason laughed. I thought it was only me that noticed that. I guess Tommy doesn't care. I wonder why she doesn't have one. Most women wouldn't want to show off a body that didn't have a navel."

"Maybe it was an 'outy', and she wanted an "inny". Maybe there was a surgery that eliminated it. Who knows?"

"Look, Jason, no matter what we see or hear, we are lucky to have this boat. It is perfect for what we want to do. I do wish that they would come above decks and contribute to our speculations."

Nara and Tom came up to the deck and stood with them at the helm. It was awkward. Were they fooling around below? It was none of their business, really, but quite inappropriate, if they were.

"Look ahead, there!" said Nara in a louder voice than usual. "There, around the bend...the U-shaped tree branch!"

The boat continued to head in that direction, following the curve in the river. It was enormous, stripped of bark and white from the sun. There was only the remains of a kayak rental. It was a tattered shack with a ripped sign, probably the effects of a storm or lack of customers.

"That's where I got in the water. I rented the kayak there." She pointed. "I didn't go very far before finding the rogue."

They decided to anchor overnight and get a good night's rest. There was no sense running out of light when their first sighting of the rogue was so important.

The next morning, Tom woke with Nara at his side. They had had their happy ending after a mutual massage the night before. The sun was glittering on the water. Nara jumped up and threw on shorts and top. "I will get the coffee going and make something for us to eat before we get underway. Don't go back to sleep, Tom. Come on. Today is the day we make history!"

In the kitchen, mid-decks, Ivan had already made the coffee and was having a cup at the table, looking at the map and checking the sonar reading. She entered the room, surprised to find him awake.

"Well, hello, Nara. You cooking this morning?" He grinned. He had washed his salt and pepper hair and beard in a manly soap that spiced the air. He was dressed in khaki shirt and pants, like a proper adventurer. "Are you ready to explore?"

"Yes and yes. Eggs? Bacon?" She got out the pans. "I'm going below to get a portion of my seafood mix for breakfast. I swear it gives me super strength. Want some?"

"No thanks. I don't even like sushi. Just eggs and sausage, if we stocked any. I'll see to the toast." The others joined them, Jason rubbing sleep from his eyes. He had too many Jack Daniels night caps.

She returned with raw oysters and several prawns.

"I don't know how you can eat that in the morning," said Tom.

"I told you, I love seafood. How are your eggs?"

"You are the perfect cook. After we clean up this mess, let's get going," said Ivan, eager for the first thrust at a successful entry.

"Stifle your high anxiety. We have to go over the check list of equipment that we will need first." Tom pulled out the list. "Everything we will need has to be piled on this table before we start the engine."

"All right. You read, we will assemble," said Jason, pouring his second cup of coffee, eyes barely visible above dark bags.

"This mission requires abstinence from alcohol, Jason. Just like sobriety makes great athletes, it also makes great scientists." Nara was becoming less liked now by Jason. He nodded.

It was agreed that Nara take the helm. She supposedly knew the way. She started the engine, they hauled up the anchor, and off went The Ocean Glory. All eyes sought the opening as they sped past the rental shack.

Tom commented, "I think it is really unusual that the only wildlife seems to be birds, and not many at that. There are more rocks jutting out here, be careful rounding the bend."

Nara dodged a big boulder at top speed. The boat was now lifting up out of the water splashing the crew members and the deck. They held tight to the railings as Nara slowed down a bit to take the broad turn.

"It shouldn't be long now," she said. "On the left bank was a flat area of marsh that widened into a circular gateway comprised of woven bamboo grass. It was really quite amazing."

"It's been a few years since then. I hope the landmarks are still the same," said Jason, as she slowed the speed even more. The Ocean Glory rocked capriciously as the water was a little wilder at this spot. Rivulets ran faster. All eyes were focused on the left bank.

Sure enough, the flora on the banks changed to a mushy bright green flotilla, undulating in the current.

"I think this is it. We are going to have to get closer and maybe push the boat through the narrow entranceway to the expanse of the rogue," she said.

"Aye-aye, Captain." She cut the engine and riding the swells, the boat stopped.

Tom leaned forward with his binoculars. "The marsh is littered with fish skeletons. I guess there are more birds than we thought. Something is eating them…cleaning the flesh to the bone."

Ivan said, "What are we waiting for? Let's head into the marsh and find that circle." He elbowed Nara out of the way. "I'll take over now."

"We have to vote on this, Ivan. You aren't leading this team by yourself." Jason was irritated.

"I say we all say 'aye'. Why should we delay what we've been dreaming of for years?"

They all nodded in agreement to proceed. Ivan took the wheel. They turned toward the obscure channel and fought through long blades of reeds and river grass underneath the surface. The engine sputtered, getting tangled.

"Stop!" called out Jason. We're going to have to push through. We can't risk damaging the rotors."

"I am the best candidate to go under and pull off the grasses from the propellers. I can stay under a long time." Nara prepared to dive over the side into the marsh water, again without a stitch of clothing on.

"Wait!" called Tom. "We don't know what's down there."

She had already splashed into the marshy green, slimy water and disappeared. They expected bubbles, but there were none. The boat shuddered when she pulled the grasses off the blades. She was under about twenty minutes. Suddenly, she emerged, grinning. "All clear, but I suggest we use the bamboo poles to push her along until we get out of the weeds."

Tom helped her aboard. The men tried not to look. Her breasts were round with pink areolas and nipples. Her skin was white and sleek. Ivan and Jase were thinking the same thing...what she would be like in bed. Lucky Tom.

With no inhibitions at all, she pulled on her shorts, tucking her breasts securely into the halter top.

Ivan pursed his lips. "Wow! You are something!"

Tom hugged her to him. "Let's get the poles. They're below decks."

Like a segment from the movie, "African Queen", the four crewman pushed hard to move The Ocean Glory through tough weeds, groaning and sweating under the hot sun.

"At least there are no leeches, or bees," said Ivan.

"Don't speak too soon. We don't know what is on this mysterious branch. There doesn't seem to be much, though. It's like the ecology is different now. I wonder what that white thing was in the water way back. It almost looked like someone threw a bathtub in the water." Jason stopped a moment to rest. The boat was heavy due to its size, even though it was lighter than most others in comparison.

"Keep to it. We are making progress," said Nara, taking a deep breath. Her skin was wrinkling, drying out. With that, she swooned over, dropping her bamboo pole in the water.

Tom rushed to her side and tried to revive her. She was dead in his arms as he carried her below. He called over his shoulder, "Keep pushing. I'll be back when she's okay."

Her lips moved. "The tank. I need…"

He carried her to the room that housed the giant tank of cold water. She was limp. He was frightened. At the top of the ladder, he let her body fall into the volume of water. She went to the bottom and lay there, not moving. He stripped his clothing and jumped in to be with her. When he reached her, he tried to lift her to the surface. She quickly revived, pulled off her shorts and wrapped her legs around him. Her hips gyrated slowly, rubbing his exposed genitalia. She was all right. She wanted sex. He was willing. Even though the water was cold, he was able to function. Her face expressed ecstasy when he ejaculated into her. Then, she pushed him away and grabbed his hand, pulling him to the ladder.

When they broke the surface, she said, "Hurry. We have to get back to the rogue."

He fumbled for his clothes. She was already back in her skimpy outfit, heading up the steps. He followed her lead, fighting another hard-on, watching her climb the rungs ahead of him.

Jason and Ivan were still pushing hard, faces red, sweat pouring down their faces and shoulders. They turned to Tom and Nara.

Jase asked, "Are you all right, Nara?"

"I am fine. I just needed hydration. How are we doing?" she asked, fishing her pole back from the surface of marsh. She began to push with new strength.

Tom said, "Look, we're almost through this muck, and there is the circle of bamboo straight ahead."

"This is it. This is the entranceway to waters unknown. It looks silver from here, like a clear metallic lake."

Once free of the entanglements in the marsh channel, they turned on the engine and glided toward the circular gate. A wall of vines fell behind them, obscuring the way into the rogue.

Nara looked like a graceful statue staring out onto the lake. Ivan was taking photographs, and Jason was holding steady on the wheel. Tom was getting the skiff ready to be lowered so they could row ashore and leave The Ocean Glory anchored away from the silver sand beach.

"Whoa! What is that in the center of the lake?" asked Ivan, increasing the zoom on his lens. "It looks like a vortex. Look, the water is starting to spin."

The calm water beneath them started to undulate in small ripples. The boat began to turn. Thick, silver clouds descended over the water. It wasn't mist, it was a thick vaporous cloud cover. They couldn't see a thing, it was that thick. Shiny white globes bobbed up and down. They drifted toward the craft from the beach. There were bubbles that made a plopping sound when they broke.

Jason said, "I can't see anyone in front of me, but I do see globes."

Ivan let out a scream. "They have eyes! They are heads. Their bodies are underwater!"

Tom shrieked, "God Almighty! What are they, and what do they want?" He stopped preparing the skiff. He heard a whirring sound of water getting louder. "They look human, but are plug-ugly."

Tom felt for Nara's soft white hand. He tightened his fingers around it, but she pulled it away, and they heard a splash. She was gone. The clouds dispersed, revealing the whirlpool had widened enough to take down the boat. They saw her swimming towards the vortex, deliberately.

"Come back!" Tom screamed, helplessly watching her spin around the sides of the spinning funnel of water.

They could see now. The bobbing heads were gone. She was gone. The funnel lost power and calmness came over the water again.

Jason grabbed Tom, who was foolish enough to attempt to go after her in the water. "We'll get her back, Tom, but not this way. Drop anchor, Ivan. We don't want to cross that maelstrom. It will take our boat, and we'll never get back." He yanked Tom back into the boat.

Ivan cast the anchor over the side. It took a long piece of rope before it hit the bottom. There was silence. The engine was cut off, and no birds or bubbles disturbed the air.

In shock, the men discussed their dilemma. Kinsley brought up the Jack Daniels and poured three glasses. "We need this to help us think straight and give us courage." They raised their glasses and belted down the burning amber liquid.

They stared at the spot that just a few moments ago was whirling and sucking Nara down to where? Did those things in the water want her, call her? How could she know what was going on? But, Tom didn't really know her other than in the biblical sense.

"We have got to get her back. Let's row ashore and set up camp. Maybe there is an underground passage to the bank." Tom poured himself another glass.

"Maybe those things in the water were alien beings, deciding to settle in this vast piece of unexplored Earth. Or maybe they are from the sea."

Jason said, "Let's get packing, guys. We can't stay out here." He threw a sleeping bag at Tom. "Ivan, help me gather the supplies and load the tent into the skiff."

"But, what about Nara?" Tom was agitated. "I'm going to get her. He made an attempt to climb over the rail again, and Ivan and Jason grabbed him. Jase punched him in the jaw, and he fell to the ground.

"You can't do that. We will get her back. You can count on that, but we have to go ashore and study the lay of the land. If you can't follow our command, then we'll cuff you. Do you hear me?" Jase was hot.

Ivan helped him up. Tom rubbed his jaw, tears were in his eyes. Jason patted him on the back. "This is real weird, but we will get her back." They stuffed their gear into their back packs and readied the skiff to be lowered aside the yacht. They transferred their gear and themselves into the small boat. Tom grabbed a set of oars and so did Ivan. Jason sat forward and scanned the beach for a good place to land. He pointed to a corner of the cove where there were trees for shade. They beached it there and unloaded their gear. There were still no clouds and no more bubbles. Since the whirlpool disappeared, the water became calm and all evidence of white heads with piercing dark eyes disappeared, too.

The beach had silver bits that glittered in the sun. Other than that, the beach was like any other beach where they had pitched tents and camped before.

Once the tent was set up, Ivan cocked his rifle. He looked down the barrel to the site, pointing it at the place where the vortex had appeared. The water was still calm. Nara was gone. Was she alive? What prompted her to fearlessly dive into the middle of it and be sucked down to the bottom? He also checked his PMM Makarov, Russian hand gun, and placed it in his holster.

Tom checked his sidearm, a 357 Magnum. He placed in his shoulder holster. Jason had a .38 caliber Browning, snub-nosed. Once armed, they decided to explore the interior. There was a humid mist in the forest. Each carried a back pack with provisions and temporary overnight shelter in case they didn't return to camp. Mile-ray Halogen beam flashlights were part of their staples.

Tom lingered while Jason and Ivan's machetes hacked into the tangle of vines and low branches on the perimeter. He stared out at the vast silver surface of the lake they would later call, "Danger Lake".

"Come on! We can't help her here. We have to find out where this leads. Maybe there is a connection to the funnel that took her down." Jason beckoned for Tom to hurry up.

Tom sighed, feeling guilty for not being able to stop Nara from jumping. He slowly turned and stepped faster to catch up with them.

Chapter 8

The Unfamiliar

No one had ever been there before. There was no evidence of any kind of life teeming in the trees or on the land. It was a deserted and ignored land. The sun did not shine that afternoon. It remained overcast by eerie gray low-hanging clouds. There was a smell of decay, like oysters and dampness. The ground was spongy.

"At least there are no flies or mosquitoes here. I guess there is nothing to sustain them," commented Jason as they walked along.

"You know," began Ivan, "that white" rock or whatever we suspect it might be looks like Calcium Carbonate or Calcite, CACO3. It is comprised of fragments of marine organisms – mollusks, shells, coral, algae, and even fecal debris. It is a sedentary rock that forms in warm shallow marine waters or in fresh water lakes. I think there is some salt content to this water. I will test it when we get back."

"Thanks, Professor. So, what comes of this knowledge? There doesn't seem to be any life around here on land. Nara didn't see any water creatures on her dive."

"There's something 'fishy' about Nara, Tom. I didn't want to say anything earlier, but I think she knows more than she lets on about this rogue haven."

Tom thought for a moment before speaking. He stepped over twisted whips of vines and low plant life. As they plunged forth into the interior, he answered, "I hate to admit it, but you are right. That's why she appealed to me. She was different, mysterious. Very amorous, too, I might add."

Kinsley commented, knowingly, "She seduced you. It was an easy lay. Sex will get you every time, if it's good. You are her subject. We understand, right Prof?"

Ivan grinned. "My hair might be gray, but I am still a fool for a woman and her wiles. If she weren't yours, she would be mine." He laughed. "Even without a navel."

Tom frowned. They ruined everything. He was happy until now. Had he been schnooked? It didn't matter. Maybe they were wrong. He wanted her back. The image of her nude body whirling down into the aqua labyrinth haunted his thoughts.

Noises, like heavy bags being dragged, filled their ears. They stopped. Jason signaled for them to be silent. It was up ahead. Something alive was making this noise. They crept forward at Jason's command. He signaled them to spread out. There was a clearing about a hundred yards ahead. They scoped it out with their field glasses.

Large white beings with the characteristics of snails were moving giant conch shells around in a circle. There were about five or six of these large, pupa-like creatures. They had dark piercing eyes that appeared to have no pupils. They had thick arms and flipper-like fingers. Inside the giant shells were smooth, white eggs. The men exchanged glances in surprise. The creatures didn't seem to sense their presence.

All heads turned to a tunnel opening behind the circle of eggs, or nursery. A large, white snail-like creature emerged next to Nara, who was still without clothing. Her skin was almost as white as the creature she accompanied. She left the big one's side and went over to one of the attendants. She embraced it. They didn't speak, but she knew this one. It put its flipper-like arm around her.

She could sense the presence of Jason, Ivan, and Tom. She glanced in their direction, but did not give away their location.

Tom's heart was in a turmoil. It beat loudly in his chest. The humidity was oppressive. He was panting. The others looked at him. Ivan raised his eyebrows and mouthed the words, silently, "Who is that?"

Tom shrugged. They continued to watch the ritual of the checking of the eggs. Another was put into an empty shell. One began to crack. It tortuously pushed and pried until a human arm pushed through. Its skin was white. It was small like an infant's. The top half of its form was visible. The attendants closed in, blocking the view of its hatching. Nara was among the onlookers. The large one, stood behind them, looking over their shoulders.

A dripping whelp was raised up from the broken shell for all to see. Its mouth was open, but there was no cry. It writhed around and was comforted by Nara. She took it from the attendants and handed it to the big one, who must have been a VIP of this unusual tribe. There was an overbearing smell of oysters and raw mollusks as the group followed the big one into the tunnel. Nara was the last in line. She turned to look at the others, still concealed in the bushes.

Jason signaled them to about-face and go back to the camp. They knew that Nara was all right, but they could do nothing there until they knew what they were up against.

The men retreated on their hand-made trail to the beach. When they got back, they formed a fire-ring and collected wood for the evening's light and warmth.

Tom sat on a log in front of the tent. "I hope she follows us back to explain. I know she saw us." Even under extreme conditions, he wanted to sleep with her again. He felt she was his soul mate.

"I'm confounded. What are those things, and why did they seem to know her and accept her? Who was that one that she hugged?"

"Ivan, why has no one been here before? Will we be prisoners? Are they friendly...these things?" Jason sat on a tree stump, and Ivan sat on his bedroll.

"I don't think I will sleep tonight," said Tom.

"I'm going to get a sample from the water's edge. This sand is peculiar, too. I don't know what the metal is that is interspersed with the regular sand. Earth is evolving at the insistence of Mankind.

We should have left things alone. I don't get a good vibe from these creatures. I think they are the odor we smell. They seem to be aquatic in nature, but human in their caring for the unborn, or unhatched." He picked himself up from the ground and headed toward the ocean with an empty jar and a ladle. Jason and Tom watched him. When he got almost to the water, eight white heads with angry eyes popped up and scared the pants off him. He turned and ran back, looking over his shoulder to see if he were being chased. They didn't move. Tom and Jason stood up, guns aimed. When Ivan was back at camp, they submerged. The Ocean Glory stood still in the middle of Danger Lake, calling to them.

"I guess we don't get samples. They know we are here. What happens next? Should we skedaddle? We can get in the boat and sail away home." Ivan said, sitting down, wiping anxious sweat from his brow.

"Great idea!" cajoled Jason. "A. We don't know if we can row out to the Glory, B. We came here to explore, and C. How do we find our way back?"

"No, A. Is to rescue Nara and take her back with us."

"Listen, Romeo, she's better off than we are. We are sitting ducks!"

The bushes parted, and Nara came forward. She approached the men and squatted down. She looked as beautiful as ever, but now was an exotic rarity, like those they observed.

"Tom, they want to see you. Ivan, you and Jase have to stay here. They only want to talk to you, Tom. Please, come with me. That was my brother you saw me with. I have a lot to tell you. These are my people. He wasn't developed enough to go with me to intermingle with the human population. We are part of the Conch Conversion that Warren Wild PhD started years ago."

Their eyes widened in shock at what they were hearing.

"They are peaceful…or I should say 'we'," she said and moved over to sit on Tom's lap. She stroked his hair with her white hand and kissed his cheek. His loins stirred. The others watched, suspicious of her move.

"Nara," he said, "What are you talking about? I can't believe…"

She put her fingers to his lips. They smelled of seafood. "Shush. Believe it. Listen, I have a plan to get back, all of us, but you have to do as I say and come with me now." She stood up and offered her hand to Tom, who got up and followed her into the woods. The branches closed over, prohibiting the others from seeing where they went.

Ivan said, "We have to go after them!"

Jason answered, "No, we have to wait. Didn't you hear her? She's got a plan for us all to return home. She knows what's up. We don't. Sit down and wait. I'm tired. I'm going to take a quick nap."

He pulled his cap over his eyes and lay down in the sand, using his bedroll for a pillow.

Ivan stared at the lake, the boat, then scanned the place where Nara led Tom. When he was sure that Jason was asleep, he got up and searched for a place to enter the woods. He would find them and rescue them from these strange 'people' who she deemed harmless.

Chapter 9

Conversation with Evo-Scientists

Dr. Heinrich Von Horst and his two colleagues, Clive Barrett and Remo Moss, awaited the arrival of Nara and Tom Latimer. The three sat at a crude wooden table underground in a bamboo-supported earthen cave. There were rough cabinets holding beakers and jars and instruments one would use in experiments of the flesh.

Nara and Tom entered through a parted bamboo fiber curtain.

"Ah, here they come now." Heinrich stood and stuck out his hand to shake Tom's in a greeting. He was human, of German descent. He had gray hair with mustache and beard. His eyes were bright blue. His colleagues stood behind him, in line, to shake Tom's hand.

Tom shook his hand and asked, "Who are you, sir, and what is your business? Is this some kind of laboratory?"

He laughed heartily as the others shook his hand, too. "I guess we've been here so long, we forget that no one knows of our doings. We are followers of Darwin, proving his theory by reversing it. We believe that Man came from the sea, and to prove it, we are converting Man, by way of blending the characteristics of the Conch with the lung capacity of man into sea-breathing creatures, once again. It is of the utmost importance for the longevity of the race to be able to survive in global warming, when the seas overtake the land."

Tom thought Von Horst was a nut case… truly a mad man who was taking him into his confidence, as though he couldn't or wouldn't agree with his cockamamie idea.

"Sit, sit." He pointed to a crude wooden stool. Nara stood behind him, silent.

His associates backed away and busied themselves with beakers and microscopes.

"Nara is a product of our advanced experimentation with Conch hybrids. She is the star pupil in our conversion line-up. She is as human as they get so far. Unfortunately, her brother has not evolved beyond our last issue. Two hybrids, male and female, are hatched from the same egg. They will mate if the characteristics for human water-breathers is apparent. They, of course must look and act like humans so they can infiltrate society and produce the result we expect: water-breathing humans. Nara passed the test with flying colors, in fact, she is exceptionally attractive, which gives her the breeding edge."

"We have had sexual relations, Dr. Von Horst. She told me that she could not have children."

"No, she cannot. But, she can lay eggs, you see. We have examined her and she is carrying an egg that you fertilized. The union must take place under water. When you copulated in the water, it was in our breeding tank on The Ocean Glory. That ship was designed by Warren Wild. His first hybrid was Professor Horace Nordic of Breen University. He has since died, but Nara is his successfully bred daughter. Isn't she beautiful?" He looked up at Nara. She smiled, seductively.

"Why didn't you tell me, Nara?" Tom asked, bewildered. "I don't want to be part of this experiment. It is an abomination. What are you going to do with all of the rejects? Is that what is forming the boulders in the lake? And, how do you control the vortex? Where does it lead?"

"So many questions, Thomas. I will answer them all, but first, let me show you the way to the whirlpool. There is a doorway that leads to a chamber that pulls down the water magnetically when a vacuum is created. Look, I'll show you."

Through a periscope, the surface of the lake showed The Ocean Glory anchored in the middle.

Von Horst reached for a switch on the wall, and the air began to be sucked into a pipe that led to the outside. The water started to swirl in a growing eddy.

"Stop!" Shouted Tom. "You can't take down our boat."

Heinrich flipped the switch, and the water returned calm. Air refilled the glass chamber.

"Of course. We won't do that, but we will take your cargo of seafood. Our colony thrives on it. We only have fish here, but there are sharks, like in the old colony at Conch Island."

"What about this egg Nara is carrying? How long does it take to lay a Conch egg?"

"Only a few days, son. You and your friends have to stay until it has hatched and we determine the progress made with Nara as the prize hybrid so far. You may name your children, if you like. You will have made history in the science world when we are ready to expose our findings."

Tom felt sick. He didn't picture his firstborn child to be a large, white egg in a giant sea shell.

Kinsley and Isaacs were brought into the tunnel to meet with Von Horst. He looked them over and shook hands with them. "Would you mind letting us do some tests on you for our conversion studies? I promise there is no pain or invasive procedure...just blood samples. You are in the midst of a scientific discovery that will change the world. Even if you don't believe in Darwin's theory, we need you to prove it is true."

Ivan said, "I'm game, but I do not believe it." An assistant took him to a curtained off room where he drew blood.

Kinsley stepped forward. "I hate needles, Doc; always did, but go ahead. I want my name in the papers some day for this." He went into the room when Ivan came out.

"Tom, we have saved you for last. We want to see that your DNA matches that of the breathers in the egg...the one that Nara laid."

It made Tom flinch to think she laid an egg, and it was from his sperm. Yuck! The blood drawing was quick, after which, Von Hurst told his aides to lead them to a place where they could sleep. Nara whispered to Tom as he passed through the doorway to the sleep chambers, "I will come to you later to explain. We will be leaving here in the morning."

"I don't know what to think about all of this. My main concern is to get home. I've seen enough. It's more than I expected. I can't say I'm thrilled with the advance in this huge experiment."

She took his hand and kissed it, pressing it to her cheek. "I understand."

Dr. Von Horst witnessed their intimate moment and smiled.

Tom lay on his cot, staring at the bamboo ceiling. He jumped when he heard Nara enter the room. She sat down on the cot. "Let me explain." She kissed him, and his loins stirred. He was hooked on her.

"I bought this boat so that we could all have what we wanted. I wanted to see my brother and try to free him...take him home with me. They won't let me take him. I am afraid they are going to dissect him and discard his body in the lake. That's where they throw all of their mistakes. I think that is what forms the rocks we saw; sediments of failed experiments."

He nodded, trying to comprehend the madness of her story. She wasn't totally human, but she was beautiful, intelligent, and kind. How could she have conned him like this?

"Who is that big, fat white creature you were with earlier?"

"She is the Queen Conch. My father was to be her royal consort, but he was killed. The sharks destroyed most of the original colony on Conch Island. They were water breathers."

"Where is she now? And my main question is: when are we getting out of here? I want to go home." He was nervous.

"I will tell you later how we will leave. I want to take my brother, and I want to wait until the egg hatches our offspring." She pushed him back to a reclining position. "Sleep for now. You will need your rest."

He lay back on his pillow, watching her leave through the curtained doorway. His mind was swimming with ugly thoughts of viewing the twins from the egg, soon to hatch. Would his son be a lump of skate-like flesh with black dots for eyes and flippers? Or would he look like himself and the female look like Nara? He wished he could snap his fingers and be in his own bed, never having met Nara, never having sailed down the Darlington in search of the rogue.

Tom would rather have lived in his shack alone for the rest of his life than be there. He opened his eyes and saw Ivan and Jason looking down at him. "The faster you get up, the faster we might be able to go home," said Jason. There was no coffee in the morning; no bacon or eggs. Just raw oysters and clams and boiled water. The three were led to a rough-hewn table and stools where breakfast was served to them in bowls made of carved shell. They ate with bamboo spoons.

Ivan ate with gusto. Justin toyed with the bits of sea flesh, and Tom pushed his dish away.

Von Horst entered the room. "Gentlemen, I have an announcement. The egg has hatched, and all is very well indeed. Thomas, you should be very proud this morning. I want you to come and see your children. Nara was the perfect DNA match for you. They appear to be human, even though they are water breathers. Come, come. You two are welcome to join us. We have made history! Darwin was right! We were able to reverse the process and return Man to the sea, just in time."

Tom pushed himself away from the table. His friends joined him to view the new beings. They walked through a small tunnel back to the nursery where they saw Nara and the queen Conch admiring the new additions to their hybrid species. To Tom's surprise, they looked like human babies. One was male, one was female. They were naked, not to be clothed. Nara lifted the infant boy from the shell, turned and handed it to Tom. "This is your daddy." He reluctantly took the bundle into his arms. There was a warmth inside him that accepted it as his own. Nara smiled and reached for the female twin who shared their features, but had soft, pale hair tightly curled in ringlets.

The queen looked at them both, holding their progeny. She leaned into Nara as though to say something, but no words were emitted. Nara nodded.

"She marvels at the eye color. They are green, not brown or black like former subjects were. This means a great jump in progress of conversion properties."

"What is to become of them? We can't stay here, at least Jase, Ivan and I cannot." Said Tom.

"We will take them with us and raise them as our own. Of course, we have to marry to make it all legal and inconspicuous."

The queen nodded and left the premises. Von Horst stepped forward and took a close look at the male.

"He is magnificent. Of course, we must see if he is truly a water breather. Clive, take the child to the tank and lower him into the water. Do the same with the female."

He and Barrett each took an infant from their parents' arms and headed for another tunnelway to another room.

"No!" shouted Tom. They might drown!"

"So, you do have paternal attachment to them, already. If they don't swim, they will be allowed to drown, and another experiment will be conducted. It will indicate that their longevity will be too short to live normal life spans anyway. You can inseminate Nara again in the very same tank. Another..."

"You cold-hearted, God-less bastard!" shouted Tom. Kinsley and Isaac watched in horror.

Tom ran to the chamber that held the tank. Too late. The infants were in the water, sinking to the bottom. He jumped into the tank to save them. Within a few minutes, the infants glided past him, staring at him as they swam, expertly. He tried to grab his son, but he paddled away, doing summersaults in the water. The little girl was also doing aquatic stunts; neither one of them was appearing to have difficulty breathing. They were truly water-breathing humans.

Nara splashed into the tank and played with the twins, but Tom couldn't hold his breath any longer and had to climb out, gasping.

"Excellent!" exclaimed Von Horst. "We have all the components needed to make one final cross-breeding. Congratulations to Nara and Tom for the completion of this experiment."

Tom slicked back his wet hair. "What do you have planned for them?"

"You will raise them in society, seeing to it that they marry. In this manner, the evolution will continue naturally. No more need for experimentation...no more waste of life."

"I suggest that you leave as soon as possible. Your voyage home won't take you long." He turned to Nara. "Thank you for your shipment of seafood. It is most appreciated. Maybe you can deliver more in the future, now that you have a vessel worthy of the trip. Maybe you can bring other items more appealing to the human palette, too." Von Horst was willing to let them go.

Ivan said, "Let's get out of here. We've been given the greenlight. Come on. Grab your babies and Nara and let's go!"

"I'll help you, come on," added Jason.

They passed the nursery with the aides attending eggs and other hatchlings that looked more like sea-slugs than human beings. Von Horst led them to the outside where they were taken to the beach, their camp, and their rowboat. When they reached the edge of the water, having packed their gear, eight fat white heads popped up, looking angry.

"Be gone!" shouted Von Horst. They quickly submerged, and the water turned calm. There was no whirlpool threatening them. The day was clear and bright, no low, vaporous land clouds. The stench of fresh-water mollusks and dead fish remained. The infants didn't utter a peep. Their voices had to be developed...vocal chords would develop later.

"Keep in touch. Just live a normal life as a married couple with twins. Goodbye, and thank you."

He gave Nara a big smooch, and the colony waved, including the queen Conch.

The loaded rowboat made it to The Ocean Glory. They boarded. Jason, the last person to get on board, had one leg dangling over the rail as he hoisted himself up. A shark snapped at his heels. He catapulted onto the deck. Ivan grabbed the rifle and shot it several times. Shark blood colored the water red, attracting a parade of fins heading their way. They noticed discarded hybrid conch failures floating in the water. The sharks made an about face and cruised, top-speed, toward their meal.

Jason started the engine, and The Ocean Glory headed toward a closed opening in the thicket where the exit was. The engine sputtered as the boat made way. Nara was going to dive down as she did before to untangle the rotors.

"No!" shouted Tom. "There are sharks in the water. I think they followed us here. Warmer water gives them energy and a keener appetite. You can't leave our children motherless. The channel of the Darlington connects to the Pacific. This is a freshwater shark migration. They resemble bull sharks."

The eight hybrid sentries were hurrying to the beach. Some were eaten.

Ivan explained his theory. "Hybrids create mutations...change in the norm, if they are consumed. It creates molecular augmentation by means of digestion and assimilation into the blood."

"Danger Lake and the rogue are not on the map."

Ivan said, "We've got to chance freeing the rotors. Tom, cover me with your gun. I'm going under." He prepared to jump, leaving his shoes on deck.

Nara was adamant about going. "I will go. It will be done faster. I'm smaller and can stay submerged, indefinitely. I'll be safe, just cover me."

She jumped overboard into the murky marsh. The passage was clear beyond the thick mushy grasses.

She quickly resurfaced and was helped aboard.

"We got lucky. It was easy. Now, we have to pole our way back. Hurry. There was a shark coming close to me, below."

They grabbed the poles.

"Nara, shouldn't you tend to the twins?" Tom asked.

"No, they're fine. I put them into the tank."

He ran down the steps and saw them playing underwater, shrimp shells littered the floor of the tank. He watched them, proudly, amazed at their outstanding abilities.

"Latimer! Get up here. Sharks are after our poles. Help!"

Tom shot up the steps and fire shots at two medium-sized sharks. One pole was chewed in half.

"It almost pulled me in!" yelled Ivan.

The boat moved more easily without the seafood barrels stowed below.

Sharks followed. The channel was opening up ahead. When it joined the vast main vein of the Darlington, the outboard allowed them to outrun the finned predators.

Jason threw down his pole. The others looked up at the white thundering current that churned the river that would take them home. The boat zipped out into the main stream.

Ivan used field glasses to see the sharks turning around far behind them, heading back to their feeding ground in the waters of Danger Lake. With cast-off flesh bits, the sharks would over-populate and go rogue. They might even evolve to become air-breathers, threatening the colony on land. Von Horst and his fellows were in danger.

Tom made up his mind that he was never going back. He had until the twins reached maturity to observe any grandchildren, praying in advance that no throw-back freaks would be birthed by egg.

Nara sat quietly, enjoying the splash of water from the speed of The Ocean Glory. She signaled Tom to follow her below decks. They saw the two newborns asleep in the corner of the tank at the bottom.

"Help me put them in their sleeping crates. They must breathe air as well as water."

They retrieved the infants who remained asleep and settled them in padded crates.

"Come with me," said Nara.

"No. No more underwater union. From now on, its land sex only." He ran up the steps. It was hot. Ivan was drenched with perspiration. Jason was dousing himself with a water bottle.

"Hey, Tom, how about taking the wheel?"

"Sure. I can handle this. We're halfway there, why don't you rest in the shade?"

Kinsley flopped into a lounge chair under the awning. Ivan went below. Tom studied the map, looking for the U-shaped branch.

Nara met Ivan at the bottom of the stairway. She pressed her nude body against him. He was aroused.

"Let's take a dip in the cool tank. Come on. Get rid of your sweaty clothes and jump in with me. It's so, so cool. Come on."

She pulled his big calloused hands toward the tank room. He hadn't engaged in sex for ten years, but he was eager to be seduced by this beauty.

She descended the ladder first, kicking away from it, and doing the backstroke, leaving her globular breasts shining like wet melons on her white body.

He dove in and did two laps with an overhand stroke. They collided in the middle of the tank. Nara reached for his genitals and squeezed his strong erection. He gasped, delighting in her boldness. She positioned herself for entry. He wasted no time accommodating her to his full potential.

Jase got up to go to the head. "Back in a flash," he said to Tom. "Gotta go. Want a drink?"

"Yeah, sure." He didn't notice that Ivan was absent. He assumed that Nara was checking on the babies.

Kinsley took a leak in the bathroom then looked into the tank room. The door was closed. When he saw Ivan penetrating Nara, he cried out, "What in hell are you doing?"

Ivan kept on going as though he didn't hear him. First, Jason was shocked, then aroused. This was one wild scene.

Tom yelled from the upper deck, "Hey, what am I, the chauffeur? Where did everybody go?" He looked over his shoulder noticing he was alone.

"You two get out of there now!" shouted Jase.

Tom heard loud voices from below decks. He cut the engine and cast the anchor.

Ivan and Nara disengaged and climbed out of the tank. Jason watched them from the door.

He looked at Ivan with a hostile glare. "Have you no scruples? Get dressed and get on deck." He threw him his clothes. Ivan complied with no comment. Nara pulled on her clothes, also and was silent.

"Tom thinks you are his woman," said Jase.

"Let's go." She pushed past him and went up the steps after Ivan. Jason grabbed two beers and went up on deck.

"Here," he said, handing one to Tom.

"What took you so long? Is everything all right with the babies?"

"They'll sleep for hours. They're fine. I was just hydrating. I feel so much better."

Ivan stood at the rail, grinning ear to ear.

What meant something to the men meant nothing to Nara. She was more animal than human...a dedicated hybrid whore for the good of science. She smiled with her secret, standing at Tom's side, pretending to help him steer.

The U-shaped branch appeared at the bend in the river. The tattered sign of the kayak rental blew in the breeze.

All hands were on deck, weary and bewildered. In high gear, Tom maneuvered around boulders and over small rapids. He yawned. "Ivan, take over, will you. It's your turn, now." He moved to the helm and gave Tom a side-long glance. He did not feel guilt, just triumph. He was totally spent and too stupid to know what he had just done.

Tom and Nara hugged and kissed in the sun, at the back of the boat. Kinsley walked up to the helm and stood next to Ivan.

"I thought more of you, Isaacs. How could you?"

"It was easy. You should try her. I'm sure she wouldn't mind. She wanted it. She's inexhaustible."

"I have more integrity than you. Don't do it again! It isn't fair to Tom."

Ivan spat out, "He doesn't deserve her, but I will back away. It sure felt good."

Jason sighed. "Well, I think Nara, although beautiful, is a user. She might break his heart."

"They're going to get married and raise those freaks below."

Chapter 10

Home

Kinsley pulled the truck around to the dock. Levine came out to welcome them back.

"Where did you go?"

Tom said, "No place that would interest you. We're docking The Ocean Glory." He scribbled off a check and handed it to him. "This should keep her for six months." Levine took the check, looked at it, raised his eyebrows, smiling, and went back to his office.

They loaded up the vehicles that carried the silent twins, who occupied cushioned whiskey crates. Levine watched them from within in his dark glasses, chewing on a cigar.

Tom told Ivan and Jason that they could stay in his rental, and he would move into Nara's house in the desert with the twins. "We'll talk later about putting our evidence together. We'll make a lot of money on our story. Of course, we keep Nara and the twins out of it."

It was agreed. Nara sat shotgun in the SUV, infants in the back seat.

Jase leaned past Ivan, who was driving, and asked Tom, "What did you name your son?"

"Pisces, sign of the fish in astrology."

"And, what did Nara name her daughter?"

Tom looked sad. "She didn't make it. Most likely the genes were defective."

Nara looked into the back seat at Pisces. He tried to coo. The other crate held the body of his dead twin sister. She was wrapped up in newspaper, like a big fish and remained nameless.

Kinsley stayed in the house with Ivan until the papers were completed and submitted to Science Digest. Ivan stayed in the house, drinking heavily, dreaming of another encounter with Nara, but it never happened.

Nara and Tom had a civil ceremony in Parchment Prairie. He continued to work for the cement plant, and Pisces was raised as a spoiled, only child with special talents, home-schooled by his mother.

Tom thought of the peril of sharks invading Darwin's hybrid colony, but that was a faraway dream that he did not want to revisit. Ivan's alcoholic sperm was too old and sparse to fertilize Nara's egg and produce two other living beings. Ivan never knew what consequence could have come from their interlude in the tank, nor was he sober enough to care.

Tom watched Pisces grow, swimming, always swimming for hours, underwater. It would be a long time before he would reach puberty and impregnate a human female. Then, it would be time to return to the colony with the next advanced subject who might hatch a perfect egg.

It wouldn't be easy getting Pisces' mate to the colony, explaining about the egg she carried, and that it was for the good of science and the survival of Mankind; but there was plenty of time to enjoy his son and continue loving Nara, his beautiful, sensuous wife. No more hanky-panky underwater, though. He learned his lesson; she did her duty. Her father, Professor Horace Nordic, would be proud of her, had he survived.

www.ingramcontent.com/pod-product-compliance
Lightning Source LLC
LaVergne TN
LVHW041543060526
838200LV00037B/1115